HIGHWAY OF
LOST LOVE

A Novella by
Kevin C. Malin

P.O. Box 15201
Seattle, WA 98115

Publisher's Note: This is a work of fiction. Names, characters, places, and incidents are a product of the author's imagination. Locales and public names are sometimes used for atmospheric purposes. Any resemblance to actual people, living or dead, or to businesses, companies, events, institutions, or locales is completely coincidental.

HIGHWAY OF LOST LOVE/ Kevin C. Malin. — 1st ed.
ISBN 978-0-9986289-0-5

To Robert and Natalie Malin

Chapter 1

Hard at Work

On an early Saturday morning I was in my apartment working on a new television script. The network was expecting the final draft in a week so I had to stay focused and not get distracted. Equipped with an adequate supply of caffeine and plenty of determination, my fingers danced upon the keyboard, making the words sing like the sweet notes coming from Chet Baker's golden trumpet. I was really in my element, deep in a dreamlike trance, hearing distant voices and unspoken thoughts, digging up a vast storehouse of feelings and emotions, when all of a sudden I felt a pair of warm, comforting hands rest upon my shoulders causing my mind to drift back and forth from fantasy to reality before finally settling in on the person standing behind me. It was no use trying to type another word; my train of thought vanished in an instant.

"Hey, Johnny, I better get going."

"What's the rush?"

"I want to get home before my husband becomes suspicious."

"Ah, let him. A little jealousy can't hurt."

"That's easy for you to say, you're not married."

"Listen, Angela, marriage is a dangerous trap, and the quickest way to escape it is to run into the arms of a lover."

"You are so full of shit, Johnny!"

Angela went to grab her coat and handbag, and I turned toward her with a sense of disappointment as I wasn't prepared for her to leave just yet. "I only say that because I care about your well-being."

"Oh, Please! All you care about is getting your rocks off. Do you really want to hear about my personal life?"

"Not really."

"I didn't think so. I'll see you later."

Angela headed for the door and I tried to think of something to prolong her stay.

"Hey, Angela!"

"What?"

"Come here for a second."

"What is it?"

"I want to show you something."

Angela grudgingly walked up to me and I stood up to face her and unzipped my pants. "Say hi to Joe Sunday."

"Oh, Johnny, you are such a weirdo!"

I laughed at her reaction, but could tell that she was amused by my antics. "I couldn't help it!"

"Yeah, sure you couldn't."

Angela headed for the door again, but I didn't mind because I already blew my load and needed to get back to work. I sat back down at my laptop and prepared to type out some more words.

"Give my regards to your husband."

"Fuck you, Johnny!"

I looked over at her and gave her a warm smile. "Next week, same time?"

"Yeah, pencil me in for next week. At least you're good for something, Johnny Curtis."

I could always count on Angela for a quickie. She had a sharp tongue, but if the situation arose, she knew how to put it to good use. As soon as Angela left I took a sip of coffee and started typing away, drifting back to that old familiar place known only to me, catching my groove once again, giving those words a smattering of grease, grime, and love, and piling on a hot lusting heap of undivided attention. That's how writers make love when a real person's not around, well that's what they say anyways.

Chapter 2

A Mixed Bag of Surprises

With Angela gone, I made good progress on my script, grabbing the elements of style out of thin air and gracing the pages with phrases and clauses, question marks and exclamation points, and even employing the lonely, but often misunderstood semicolon. Things were really coming together nicely, but then my damn cell phone rang, that annoying piece of modern-day equipment!

"Hey, what's up?"

"Johnny, you must come down here at once!"

"Huh?"

"I'm in the bar at Singer's Deli, there's no time to lose!"

"What is it, Charles?"

"I can't tell you over the phone, it's something that must be experienced in person."

"Well can't it wait? I'm working on my script right now."

"No! Absolutely not! So drop your cock and grab your socks and get your butt down here this instant and you'll find out everything there is to know about it. Veronica and Percy are already on their way, and I won't take no for an answer!"

"Okay! Okay! Cool your jets, Charles. I'll get there as soon as I can."

"Good! And don't dilly-dally."

Highway of Lost Love

When it comes to Charles everything's always an emergency. He expects people to drop what they're doing at a moment's notice and rush over to meet him somewhere. The man's never held a job and has no concept of what it's like to work for a living. His father was in the steel business and made out pretty well, so a life of privilege is all that Charles has known. It's easy to picture him as some English aristocrat drinking cognac and playing croquet on the lush grounds of his countryside manor and calling out to me from a distance, "Tally-ho, old bean! The big push is on!"

I drove as fast as I could to see what all the hoopla was about. The sooner I could finish up with Charles, the sooner I could head back home and work on my script. Singer's Deli on Melrose was about a 30-minute drive from my apartment in West Hollywood. It was one of those New York-style delis where the walls are covered with photos of celebrities and where the sandwiches are so big you can't get your month around them.

When I entered the deli I headed back to the bar area looking for Charles. The place was crowded and noisy with servers holding big circular trays of food rushing in all directions through the labyrinth of tables.

"Johnny! Over here!" Charles called out.

I spotted Charles and Veronica in a corner booth and headed over there.

"Ahh, you made it record time! How are you, my good friend?"

"I'm doing fine. How are you, Charles?"

"Splendid! Simply splendid!"

"Hello, Johnny," Veronica said in a deliberately slow and sexy voice.

"Hi, Veronica, you're looking good."

"Just good? Or am I hot?"

"You're smokin' hot, Veronica!"

"Thank you, Johnny, that's just what I wanted to hear."

"Percy shall be arriving shortly," Charles announced. "Johnny, I hope you don't mind, but I took the liberty of ordering a couple of bottles of wine for us all."

"Not at all."

"Here, let me pour you a glass." Charles picked up the wine bottle and filled up my glass with a nice red table wine. "A little more, Veronica?"

"You know I like to drink, Charles. You keep pouring and I'll keep drinking."

"That's my girl!" Charles said exuberantly as he filled up her glass.

Veronica was the free-spirit of the group and would have a go at almost anything fresh and exciting. Pleasure was her motivator and variety, her sustenance. If given the opportunity, Veronica would go to bed with one lover and wake up with another, and she wouldn't have it any other way. She believed in following one's intuition and often spoke about the importance of living life with passion and purpose.

"I must try everything once, and if not once, then twice," she liked to say. "There's nothing more stimulating and nothing more desirable than allowing yourself to be seduced by someone to the point where your mind drifts between states of dreaming and awakening. And if you give in to your true self, you'll find that there's no difference between the two."

I took a sip of wine and glanced over at the table next to us where an older couple was sitting quietly and nibbling on their food. They stared at each other with expressionless faces as if they ran out of things to say long ago. *"Holy shit!"* I thought to myself. If that's what happens after 50 years of marriage, I want no part of it.

"Ahh, here comes Percy!" Charles announced. "Perfect timing!"

"Hello, everyone!" Percy said enthusiastically.

"Nice to see you, Percy," Veronica said.

"Likewise, my dear, Veronica."

"Hi, Percy."

"Hello, Johnny, how's the script coming along?"

"It's almost done."

"That's fantastic! Maybe you'll win an Emmy this year."

Charles picked up the wine bottle and filled Percy's glass and then we all said cheers and clinked glasses. However, Percy went a step further and offered up a rather colorful and passionate toast: "All for one and one for all! Let us drink heartily to the Knights of the Garter and remember the valor and bravery of a young man from Wales: Edward of Woodstock, the Black Prince!"

Percy was one of the busiest and most respected actors in the Los Angles theatre scene. He took his craft seriously and put his whole being into the parts he played. Even when he wasn't on stage he always seemed to be performing before an audience, and we were no exception.

It was quite by accident that we all ended up in the same city on the west coast. We met each other in English class at Evanson University in New York and became fast friends. Back then our restaurant of choice was the Flapper Dapper Alley on Sullivan Street where we'd hang out after school and talk about our lives and careers and our relationships. I remember we used to camp out in the same corner booth because a poster of our favorite book *The*

Great Gatsby was mounted on the wall above us. We used to dream about living in the fictional town of West Egg on Long Island where Jay Gastsy had his mansion. Our classmates and the people who knew us used to call us the *Eggs of Sullivan Street*, but I always thought that it was a pretty silly name.

"I think I'm up for another drink!" Veronica said. "Fill 'er up, Charles!"

"Certainly!"

"So Charles, tell us why you dragged us all down here."

"Patience, Johnny, patience. I was just about to get to that."

Charles picked up a paper bag that was lying beside him and pulled out a small figurine and held it up for all to see. "Feast your eyes on this little treasure!" he said gleefully.

"Wow! That's beautiful!" Veronica remarked.

"It sure is!" Percy said. "Tell us about it!"

"This, my friends, is a marble statue of the goddess Athena. It's over two thousand years old!"

"Where did you get it?" I asked.

"My Uncle Alfred picked it up when he was in Greece last month. He just gave it to me yesterday. It's a priceless antique."

We passed the statue around the table and each one of us examined it closely as if it were a piece that belonged in a museum.

"I thought it was illegal to own antiquities such as this," I said.

"The laws regarding the trading in antiquities are quite vague. This piece probably falls into some sort of gray area. Anyways, no one's gonna miss one little statue."

Charles carefully placed the figurine back in the bag and we all thanked him for sharing it with us.

"Can I refill your wine glass, Johnny?"

"I should be heading back now, Charles."

"Take another drink first, then you'll be good for the road."

"All right, one more," I relented.

"That's the spirit, Johnny! A little alcohol in your veins will do wonders for your libido," Percy said.

"Is that so?"

"I can vouch for that," Veronica chimed in. "Whenever I invite a man over to the house, I make sure I have plenty of wine around. And then, when he's good and ready, I put him to work in my private garden."

"Well said, Veronica! Well said," Charles interjected.

That Veronica was some lady, all right. Smart, independent, self-assured, a passion for adventure, and a high sex drive. Why, she could lure any man to her pad with just a smile and place him under her spell with a wink. A seductress, first class!

"By the way, Johnny, did you hear the news?" Charles asked.

"No. What news?"

"Veronica's now a member of the Owls!"

"You're an Owl?" I asked in total surprise.

"Yep! I am an Owl!"

"And she's not just any Owl!" Charles added. "She's an English Owl! Isn't it wonderful!"

"Yes, wonderful," I answered without much emotion. "When did you become an Owl?"

"I just got initiated into the group last week."

"Nobody said anything to me about it!"

"We couldn't tell anyone until she was formally inducted into the order," Charles explained.

I remember Charles telling me that it was virtually impossible to get into the Owls, and the only reason that he got in was because of his father's connections. So when I heard that Veronica had become an Owl it completely caught me off-guard.

"Doesn't it feel good to be an Owl?"

"It sure does, Charles. Becoming an Owl has changed my life!"

"Really? In what way?" I asked.

"When you become an Owl, you become part of a special and exclusive community, like a second family, a second home, a feeling of unconditional love. It's a life-changing experience where you're immersed in something greater than yourself."

"That was absolutely beautiful, Veronica. I would truly be lost if I hadn't become an Owl." Percy commented.

"Wait a minute! You're an Owl too?"

"Oh, yes. I just celebrated my one-year anniversary as an Owl."

"I didn't know that!"

"Well, now you do know."

"You're all Owls! Except for me!"

"Don't take it too hard, dear boy, it's only a club," Charles said trying to console me.

"Yes, but I'm not a member of it!"

"Well, aren't you a member of the National Butterfly Society? Now none of us are members of that club."

"Yes, but anyone with $25 can join it!"

"But it's still a club, Johnny. We can't all belong to the same organizations; we all have different interests."

11

"Yeah, I suppose you're right."

"I am right!"

The three of them went on and on about how great it was to be an Owl and how it had changed their lives and other assorted mumbo jumbo. I tried to ignore them, but their conversation about the wonders and virtues of being an Owl really got to me. "Oh, this is too much!" I shouted. "Does anybody want to go see a movie tonight?"

"It'll have to be another time," Johnny. "There's an Owl meeting tonight," Veronica mentioned.

"Yes, another time would be better," Charles said. "Unfortunately, tonight's not a good night for any of us. An Owl has an obligation to attend all Owl meetings."

Being snubbed by my friends really burned me up. I felt excluded and marginalized and became desperate to belong. "How does one become an Owl?"

"It's not just a matter of becoming an Owl, Johnny, it's a way of life," Charles asserted.

"It is the way," Veronica added.

"Precisely!" Percy piled on.

"Well, I want to be an Owl!" I pleaded.

My request to become an Owl was met with resistance and excuses, and Charles tried to make it sound like it wouldn't be the right fit for me. "In order to become an Owl, one must practice honesty, humility and kindness, support one's fellow brothers and sisters through thick and thin, and adhere to the Code of English Owls as conceived in Manchester in the year 1178 AD. An Owl must always be prepared to go above and beyond the call of duty."

"I can do that!"

"And it takes a sponsor to get in."

"You can be my sponsor!"

"I don't know," he said with reservation."

"What do you mean *you don't know*?"

Charles seemed to have doubts about my qualifications and about how much pull he had with the leadership council. "Getting into the Owls is as difficult as getting into Fort Knox," he stated.

"Oh, come on! You must know the right people to talk to."

"They might not listen to me."

"You can try!"

"I'll see what I can do, but I can't promise anything."

Chapter 3

Afternoon Refreshments

After enduring an exhausting session of bullshit with my snobby friends, I needed a little cheering up, so I headed to Santa Monica to visit a good friend of mine. It was a typical day at the shore, partly cloudy, mid-60s, old Russian men playing chess, girls in short shorts and skimpy t-shirts rollerblading down the bike trail, tourists taking in all the scenery and hanging out at restaurants and bars, and people walking along the pier eating ice cream and taking photographs. With all its wonder and all its enchantments, the ocean called for me, but I had other things in mind. So I drove on by without any reluctance or regret and eventually found myself in the place I had hoped for.

"Kiss me again, Johnny."

"Okay."

"Keep moving"

"This way?"

"No, that way."

"Is this what you want, Jessica?"

"Yes, that's what I want, Johnny, so stop talking and keep doing what you're doing."

I learned the art of kissing from an East German girl whom I met back in high school. She knew her craft well and taught me the ways of love.

"Mmm . . . ohhh . . . yes, that's just what I needed."

Yes, that's just what Jessica needed all right, and that's just what I needed too. Lying next to her in a soft bed with no clothes on was the best remedy for my anxiety. When you reach the limits of passion through body-to-body contact and meeting lips so soft and so inviting and so captivating, it would be virtually impossible to break away from such a position, save for the World Series or the Super Bowl, but other than that, I can't think of a more valuable and rewarding activity.

"You sure made Joe Sunday happy," I joyfully told Jessica.

"Who's Joe Sunday?"

"This is Joe Sunday."

"Flying at half-mast, I see."

"That's where you come in. It's your patriotic duty to raise the flag."

"You sure have a way with words, Johnny."

"What can I say? It's my profession. And I do my best work in bed."

"I'll be the judge of that!"

I first met Jessica about six years ago at a private party in Pacific Palisades. We happened to strike up a conversation about movies and found that we both enjoyed independent and foreign films. After seeing each other from time-to-time, we found that we had other things in common as well.

"It's nice being able to just drop in on short notice."

"I love it when gentlemen callers come to the house unannounced. I'm glad I was home."

"Jessica, you didn't finish your sandwich."

"I can always eat it later, Johnny. It's just a sandwich. Right now other things are more appetizing to me."

"I'm glad we could put your bed to good use this afternoon. I feel right at home here."

"Oh, yeah! I wouldn't kick you out of bed for eating crackers."

Jessica looked into my eyes pensively, then looked out the window where the palm trees were swaying ever so slightly in the gentle wind.

"You know, Johnny. I think we could be good together."

"Yeah?"

"Yeah, but I don't think you're ready to settle down in a committed relationship."

"I don't know, maybe I am."

"Johnny, you're always on the move."

"I like adventure, Jessica. What's wrong with that?"

"But what are you looking for?"

"Nothing in particular. I just like experiencing new things and living in the moment."

"But wouldn't it be nice to wake up next to a hot-blooded woman each morning?"

"The same one or a different one?"

"Shut up, Johnny, I'm trying to be serious for a minute."

I laughed at Jessica's reaction and thought my witty comeback was one of the best lines I'd ever come up with. And it did put a smile on her face which showed me that she did understand my sense of humor.

"You say the craziest things sometimes," she said while shaking her head.

"Well . . . "

Jessica seemed to get over her moment of melancholy and looked at me in a more invigorating way. She had that ability and inner-strength to not let things bother her for long and to move on to more productive things.

"Come a little closer, Johnny." She paused for a moment then looked up and down my body with a fine eye. "You've gained a little weight since I last saw you."

"You think so?"

"I should know. Remember, I'm a doctor. Are you getting enough exercise?"

"I try to."

"You know, Johnny, losing a little weight in the gut does have its benefits, especially in the bedroom."

"Are you trying to tell me something, Jessica?"

"Just a little friendly advice, that's all. Don't take it personally."

Yeah, right. How could I not take it personally? She basically just told me that my performance wasn't up to snuff.

"Johnny, you seem a little down today. Is there something bothering you? I hope it's not what I said."

"Well, you did hurt my feelings a little."

"I'm sure you'll get over it. But I do detect something else going on."

"Is it that obvious?"

"It doesn't take a psychologist to tell if something's the matter. Now what is it?

"Oh, I just learned that one of my best friends is an Owl."

"What do you mean *an Owl*?"

"My friend Veronica has become a member of the English Owls."

"What the hell is that?"

"It's one of those societies like the Elks or the Eagles."

"So what's the problem?"

"Well . . . don't you see? All my friends are Owls except for me!"

"Who the fuck cares?"

"Well, I care!"

It was obvious that Jessica just didn't get it. She didn't understand what it felt like to be the only person amongst a group of friends excluded from a club. And on top of that, knowing that your friends kept it a secret from you.

"These groups are just cults. Who needs that sort of thing? You should be happy you don't belong to a group like that."

"Yeah, maybe you're right,"

"I am right! Now take your mind off that garbage and give me your full attention. I've only got 15 more minutes before I have to head back to the office. Now kiss me while I'm still in the mood."

I didn't make a move and was still taking in what Jessica said to me. I knew she was right, but I wasn't ready to accept that fact.

"Stop sulking and kiss me!" she demanded. Kiss me like you mean it!"

I snapped out of it and regained my confidence. I kissed her like I meant it, and for good measure, I gave her my special super squiggly, which she always seemed to enjoy. It's an old trick I learned from a girl I met at a bagel shop in Montreal.

"That was good, Johnny. Now go down on me!"

"What?"

"You heard me! Go down on me!"

"You're not the boss of me!"

"Do it! . . . that's right, Johnny . . . oh, yes! . . . oooh, I love what you're doing.

She loved it, I loved it, and it all went by much too quickly. That's how it always happens. When you look back at a particular moment in time, it always seems so brief, and with each passing year, it becomes a footnote of a faded memory from a past life.

Chapter 4

It's Yesterday Once More

I got up early the following morning and felt like doing something fun and crazy, so I called up a dear friend of mine and headed down to his place in San Clemente. The radio kept me company for a good part of the way, but the further I drove from the city, the weaker the signals became. And then, just when everything faded into the static, I heard a mysterious station sending Morse Code. I figured it was probably coming from a high-powered military station at Camp Pendleton, but following the Morse Code transmission, a woman came on the air with an announcement. "This is Retro Radio Girl back from a long slumber playing the hits of the 70s and 80s, but first, a quick message to those traveling alone: "The long sobs of the violins of autumn hurt my heart with a monotonous languor. I repeat: The long sobs of the violins of autumn hurt my heart with a monotonous languor." Immediately following the message, she played *Yesterday Once More* by the Carpenters, and the moment the song ended, the radio signal faded out. I listened to the static for several more minutes hoping that the station would fade back in again, but it never did come back, and Retro Radio Girl remained lost in the ether.

Man, the moment you leave the city, the stranger the radio formats become! Not that there aren't any good stations outside of L.A., but c'mon, people, why not up the power a bit so we can hear some good music while taking a road trip? Anyway, I made it to my friend's home in record time and parked out front next to the big old maple tree.

Chapter 5

Poetic Justice

"Come on in, Johnny!"

"Hi, Florence, nice to see you!"

I gave Florence a kiss on the cheek and she led me to the kitchen where I was quickly treated to a cup of coffee and a home-made oatmeal raisin cookie. She was a gracious host and a classy woman who knew how to make a guest feel right at home.

"I saw your name in the credits last night," she said.

"Which show was it?"

"The female detective one."

"Lacey Monahan?"

"Yeah, that's it."

"Oh, that's a repeat! The last episode aired six years ago."

"Well, it must still be popular or they wouldn't be showing it."

Florence walked over to the counter and put a cover on a casserole dish and placed it in the oven.

"I better let you go see Abe. He's down in his study."

"Okay. See you in a bit, Florence, and thanks for the cookie."

As I started to leave the kitchen, Florence called out to me, "Johnny?"

"Yeah?"

"Never mind, I'll talk to you later."

I headed down the steep wooden staircase and found Abe in his study. I knocked on the door which was slightly open and walked in. He was eating a sandwich and watching a baseball game on an old 13" black and white TV set.

"Johnny, my boy! How nice to see you!"

I gave Abe a hug and pulled up a chair next to him. He lowered the volume on the TV and swung his chair around to face me. With a big grin, he looked into my eyes and gave me a couple pats on the arm.

"You're lookin' good, kid. You must have just got laid, ha-ha."

"I try to stay active, Abe."

"Take it from me, kid, dipping your wick is the best way to staying young. Look at me! I'm 81 years old, and I can still keep up with the best of 'em."

Abe Mandelbaum was an old-time poet from Brooklyn. He knew all the great writers and poets of the day and used to give poetry workshops at the Thomas Cromwell Bookstore in the Village which is where I met him. In his younger years, Abe was a card-carrying member of the American Communist Party and used to attend their meetings, picnics and social gatherings. He was even good friends with Gus Hall who ran four times as a presidential candidate for the Communist Party. He told me that about 30 years ago he finally came to his senses and became a capitalist. We kept in touch throughout the years and he came out west with his wife at about the same time I did. He's been a guest lecturer at many of the local colleges and universities and has created a loyal following in southern

California. I've bought most of his books and he's autographed every one of them.

"How's the baseball game?" I asked.

"Ahh, I'm stuck watching those damn Yankees because they took my Dodgers away!"

I laughed at Abe's answer because it was such a typical response from an old Brooklynite. "That was a long time ago, Abe, and besides, the Dodgers are located just up the highway from you now."

"I know. I should probably get over it, but that damned Walter O'Malley was a greedy son-of-a-bitch! There was absolutely nothing wrong with Ebbets Field!"

Abe turned off the TV and let out a sigh of frustration. "Anyways, I know you didn't come over to talk about baseball. What did you have in mind?"

"Tijuana."

"Ya wanna go to Tijuana? All right, I'll go to Tijuana with ya."

Abe told his wife that we were going out for a while and that we might be back late. While he went to the bedroom to grab his things, Florence came up to me and spoke in a soft voice. "Johnny, keep him out of trouble."

"I will."

"And don't let him spend all his money."

"I won't."

Abe came back from the bedroom and grabbed his coat from the closet. "Okay, let's go."

He kissed his wife goodbye and we headed out the door.

"Be careful," she told him.

Florence gave me a concerned look and then shook her head with resignation as she closed the door behind her. I felt a little guilty for taking Abe out on a wild adventure, but once we started heading down the highway, my sense of remorse subsided and all I could think about was crossing the border and having a good time.

"Man, we're really doin' it!" Abe shouted out. "We're goin' to Tijuana and nothin's gonna get in our way!"

He rolled down his window, shoved his head out and yelled, "Hey! Hey! Get outta my way! I just come back from the U.S.A.!"

"You said it, brother!" I shouted back.

Abe couldn't sit still. He was like a little kid who couldn't wait to get through the turnstiles at the amusement park.

"Hey, I just remembered a song I wrote about Tijuana!" Abe said excitedly.

"Oh, yeah?"

"Yeah. It's something I wrote a long time ago. Ya wanna hear it?"

"C'mon, Abe, of course I want to hear it!"

"Cause I'm a little modest."

"Yeah, sure you are! I turned down the radio and gave him the cue. "Okay! Sing, brother, sing!"

> Take me to Tijuana
> Take me over there
> Take me to Tijuana
> I don't have a care.
> She told me that I'm too old to go
> She told me that I should just say no
> But she can't tell me what to do
> 'Cause I'm gonna tell her that we're through.
> Take me to Tijuana
> Take me over there

Kevin C. Malin

Take me to Tijuana
I don't have a care.
She told me I better pay the rent
Well good luck, dear 'cause my money's spent
So she sent me packing the very next day
And all I could say was hip hip hurray!
Take me to Tijuana
Take me over there
Take me to Tijuana
I don't have a care.
No, I don't have a care
No, I don't have a care

Abe hit the dash with his fingers as if it were a cymbal and shouted, "Yeah!" He smiled and then looked over at me for approval.

"Hey! Not bad, Abe."

"Ya really think so?"

"Well, I wouldn't call it a masterpiece, but it was a worthy effort."

Abe smiled and nodded with pride. He looked out at the Pacific Ocean and kept his eye on a few sailboats that were slowly heading down the coast, then he looked at his watch and became restless. "When will we be there, Johnny?"

"Soon, Abe, soon."

"That's good, Johnny, that's real good."

My reassurance was good enough to put a smile on Abe's face and he joyously burst into song:

I dream of Jeannie with the light
Brown hair.
Borne, like a vapor, on summer air;

Highway of Lost Love

I see her tripping where the
Bright streams play,
Happy as the daisies that dance
on her way

Abe was so happy that he couldn't wait to cross the border and cruise the good ol' downtown streets of Tijuana, and neither could I. According to Abe, the crumbling and dilapidated buildings gave the city a certain charm, but I always thought of the place as one big oversized dump that knows how to cast a spell on unsuspecting visitors.

Once we got past Camp Pendleton, the other towns seemed to have come and gone quickly: Oceanside, Carlsbad, Encinitas, Del Mar. Then on through San Diego and all its famous beaches: La Jolla Shores, Pacific Beach, Mission Beach, Ocean Beach, Imperial Beach. Grains and pebbles and minerals and seashells, the land of sparkling sand, shifting and shaping those venerable beaches where surfers look out and contemplate the wondrous waves under dancing rainbows that appear in the mist. Milepost after milepost our minds raced as we closed in on the border and prepared ourselves to enter another world. We didn't know what to expect, but not knowing was half the fun.

The moment we crossed the border, Abe was all smiles and laughs and could barely contain himself. It was like a reawakening of youth from those hot summer days on Coney Island where kids lined up at the shooting gallery to fire BB guns and then raced to the concessions to buy ice cream cones and hot dogs. The footprints have long been buried, but Abe could still feel his feet disappear into the cool, wet sand under waves of swirling sea foam. But that youthful zeal provided just a glimpse into the nature of a very complex individual. It was only through his poems where I discovered a man who was searching for truth and meaning on his own terms, and who laid bare the inner turmoil and contradictions that can only come from a deep awareness of human behavior, experienced and observed over a period of eight decades.

America had quickly faded from view and a new setting had taken its place. Within moments, the rules had changed and new possibilities had arisen. And Abe's face lit up like shimmering moonlight over rippling water.

"We made it, Johnny! We're actually here! Let's go check out the club scene and catch some action."

On Abe's suggestion, I headed to the Zona Norte, Tijuana's notorious red light district. He took pleasure in exploring the seedier parts of town and kept a watchful eye for a lively nightclub. When I turned the corner, I noticed a young woman walking in our direction. "There's one for ya, Abe!"

He looked at her pleasingly and commented, "Hubba-hubba!"

It started to get dark, and all the neon lights began to come on. I slowed down a bit so we could get a good look at all the different nightclubs before deciding which one to go to. After driving a couple more blocks, one finally caught Abe's eye.

"Hey! Let's check out that place!" he shouted with enthusiasm.

I read the sign on the nightclub aloud. "Cool Cat Mambo Club. Purring for you 24 hours a day!"

"How 'bout it, Johnny? How 'bout it?"

"Okay, sounds good to me, Abe."

I found a parking space a few blocks away and we headed to the club. An older man dressed in a suit and tie welcomed us with a pleasant *buenas noches, mis amigos* and opened the large wooden door inviting us in.

After entering the building, we stopped for a moment to allow our eyes and ears to adjust to the new environment. Then, as we slowly moved forward, the large ostentatious interior began to reveal itself. Thick smoke from cigars and cigarettes filled the room, neon lights and large framed posters of the mambo kings graced the walls, dozens of bottles of alcohol lined the liquor shelves up to the ceiling, and scantily-clad women in high heels navigated their way selling tobacco amongst all the hustle and bustle of the joint.

When our eyes finally turned to the main stage, we saw about a dozen naked women dancing and prowling about in the most erotic ways possible. And when they weren't dancing, they were out mingling with the customers in slightly more modest outfits. I turned to Abe to get his reaction, but for a person seldom lost for words, he just looked at me and shook his head with a pleasant smile and then went back to observing the activity.

We finally decided to sit at the bar and order a few drinks. The bartender was a young, handsome man with combed back dark hair and a mustache who worked fast and efficiently. He took our order and it wasn't long before we had drinks in our hands. Abe and I chatted about the erotic nature of the place and how there were so many beautiful women all under one roof. We were deeply entrenched in another world and no other thoughts from beyond the room had any chance of entering our minds.

A couple dancers who were walking the room made eye contact with us and came over. They greeted us in Spanish then spoke to us in English. With their arms around our necks, they invited us to go upstairs with them. Abe and I looked at each other with a smile, and we both got up at the same time and were led out of the room and up a spiral staircase to the bedrooms.

The woman I was with introduced herself as Anita. I doubt it was her real name, but that didn't matter to me. She was about 25 and had shiny black hair and wore bright red lipstick. After a little haggling, we came up with an agreeable price for the kind of activities I was interested in. Before we began our intimate adventure, she pulled out the appropriate items from her dresser which was abundantly stocked with all the necessary appliances for any flavor of intimacy. We got it on as planned and I returned to the bar about an hour later. Abe hadn't returned yet, so I watched a soccer match being played on the big screen for a while.

Another hour had passed, but there was still no sign of Abe. I started to get worried and was about to call for the manager when Abe finally appeared. He was being helped by two uniformed men, one of each side of him. The young woman he was with followed close behind. The men, who turned out to be paramedics, gently eased him onto the chair next to me. They asked him if he was okay, and when Abe nodded in the affirmative, they left the building. The young woman told him to take care of himself, gave him a gentle pat on the back, and kissed his cheek before leaving.

"Abe, what happened? Are you all right?"

Abe took a while to respond. He first needed to catch his breath and then spoke with some difficulty.

"I fainted," he told me.

"You what?"

"The girl really gave me a good working over. I mean, she was on top of me pounding away and saying all these sexual things to me and I just couldn't keep up with her. I must have collapsed and she called the paramedics."

"Oh, my God! Are you sure you're okay?"

"Yeah, I'm okay. I just over-exerted myself, that's all. At least I was able to shoot my wad, but moments after that I blacked out. The girl was nice to me though, she gave me half my money back."

"I'm sorry, Abe, this was all my fault."

"No it's not, kid. I'm a big boy. I knew what I was getting myself into. I'm just not in the shape I used to be in."

"Are you sure you don't want to go to the hospital?"

"Yeah, I'm sure. Take me home, I wanna go to bed."

We got back to Abe's house at around two in the morning. Florence came out and assisted me with getting Abe out of the car.

"I'm sorry, Florence," I said resignedly.

"Help me get him to bed, Johnny."

We put Abe to bed, and as we began to leave the bedroom, he called out to me. "Next time we'll just go for coffee."

"Sure, Abe. Take it easy and get some sleep. I'll check up on you later."

I told Florence what had happened and apologized to her again.

"I've never stopped Abe from doing what he wanted to do, but he's no spring chicken anymore. That girl could have killed him!"

"I know. I promise you it won't happen again."

"I hope he at least had a little bit of fun."

"He did, Florence. That, he did."

I gave Florence a kiss on the cheek and headed for home. Good ol' Abe; he was always one to run straight into the fire and not even think about the possibility of getting burned.

Chapter 6

Unexpected News

I got up late the following morning with lots of energy and went right to work on my script. Our little excursion to the south of the border seemed to do me some good. Sometimes you need a little diversion now and then to keep things in perspective. Man, I just couldn't stop thinking about Abe! He went down to that lively Mexican town with eyes wide open and both barrels blazing! Talk about nerve! That's why his poetry resonates from one generation to the next. And you can take that to the bank!

Anyhow, I got some really good dialogue in for the mystery episode I was working on. If you can keep 'em guessing until the last five minutes, you've done your job well. I had just taken a break from typing when my cell phone rang.

"What's up, Charles?"

"Good news, Johnny! I met with Major Grimsby this morning and things look pretty good."

"What are you talking about? Who's Major Grimsby?"

"Who's Major Grimsby?" Charles responded with surprise. "Why he's the president of the L.A. chapter of English Owls!"

"What did he say?"

"He told me that if I was willing to be your sponsor, he would grant your request to be received as a full member into the English Owls of Manchester!"

"Really? Are you serious?"

"Yes, I'm serious."

I paused for a moment to let the news sink in.

"Johnny, are you still there?"

"Yeah, I'm still here, you just caught me a little off-guard . . . so, you'd be willing to be my sponsor?"

"Yes, but there may be a stumbling block."

"What stumbling block?"

"The major said that you must be a citizen of good moral character."

"I am!! I am!!"

"I know, Johnny, I'm just joshing you."

"You're killing me, Charles! Did you tell him you'd be my sponsor?"

"Johnny, I am your connection to the wonderful and inspiring life of an English Owl. Hoo-hooooo!!"

"That's the best news I've heard in a long time! I can't believe it!"

"Believe it, Johnny. You know, it wasn't easy to get you this opportunity. The major's one hell of a tough cookie and I had to pull a few strings to soften him up a bit. There are no soft softies in the Upper House of Owls, I'll tell you. And if you ever cross one of them, you might as well kiss your ass goodbye."

"I don't know how to thank you, Charles. This sounds like a great opportunity for me!"

"Are you kidding? It's the opportunity of a lifetime! You know how many people would give their eye teeth to become a member? And just so you know, women go absolutely crazy at just the sight of an English Owl. It's like flipping a switch to an automatic turn-on."

"Really?"

"Swear to God, Johnny! You'll be on third base before you know it!"

"So what do I need to do?"

"Things are moving fast. You're initiation is scheduled for midnight tonight."

"Tonight? But I'm not prepared!"

"You've got to strike while the iron's hot, my friend."

"Yeah, but–"

"Look, Johnny, do you want to be an Owl or not?"

"Well, yeah, of course I do."

"Good! I'll pick you up at eleven."

"What should I wear?" I asked nervously.

"Put on a suit and tie, and look sharp . . . gotta run."

Charles abruptly ended our conversation and I sat in my chair in utter shock. "I'm going to be an Owl!" I said to myself. "At midnight tonight!" Overcome with joy, I walked onto the deck of my apartment and looked out at the greenbelt and admired the beauty of nature. I felt young and fresh and alive, like I hadn't felt in years. And I starting laughing for no reason too. I laughed at things that shouldn't even be funny, but everything that came to my mind all of a sudden seemed funny to me. I got so caught up in the moment that I completely forgot about what Jessica said about the group. And I just couldn't wait to show her the benefits of having an Owl in her bed. It will drive her absolutely wild! And she'll never be the same after that.

Chapter 7

And the Crowd went Wild!

Charles picked me up as scheduled and we headed to the ceremony. Along the way he filled me in on what to expect during the initiation process. The lodge was located on Sunset Boulevard, a couple blocks from the famous Blue Moose jazz club. It was a beautiful old wooden structure, three stories high, and built at the turn of the last century.

I was feeling a bit anxious as we entered the packed sanctuary. It was loud and boisterous and everyone seemed to be yakking away about something. Most members sat with their arms folded in upholstered benches of midnight blue along the periphery of the hall, while the officers of the lodge sat at special tables with velvet and gold coverings in the middle of the room. They were dressed in colorful robes, dark slacks, shiny black shoes, and red-colored fezzes with tassels. Large gold medallions were worn by the officers, and smaller-sized bronze medallions were worn by the rest of the membership.

Charles and I waved to Veronica and Percy who were seated together near a large organ at one of the far corners of the hall. We were instructed to sit in high-backed chairs placed in the center of the room facing an older man with flowing white hair and black horn-rimmed glasses. He wore a long black gown and was seated in a large wooden chair adorned like a throne. Charles whispered in my ear that the older man was Major Grimsby and to not stare at him because he didn't like people staring at him.

The major looked at his watch, then stood up and walked to the lectern which was a few feet in front of him. Upon the lectern was a wooden gavel, an oversized red leather-bound book, and a large bronze pointer to follow the text. He picked up the gavel and slowly looked around the room as if he was about to pass judgment at a trial, then sounded the gavel three times. The audience quieted down and gave the major their undivided attention.

"This assembly shall now come to order! The proceedings of the English Owls of Manchester, lodge number four twenty-two are now in session, so sayeth the president!"

The entire Owl membership stood up and broke into applause and hooted away like a flock of owls gone wild. The major enjoyed the spectacle so much, he gave out a few hearty hoots himself and then nodded in approval.

"Yes! Yes! Yes!!" the major yelled out. "Ha! That's the kind of spirit I want to hear! Yeah, baby!" Satisfied with the thunderous response he got, the major hit the sounding block twice with his gavel and the applause gradually faded and everyone sat down. When the hall became quiet, the major continued the proceedings. "I now call upon the honorable first secretary Barnaby Beale to sound the gong."

Barnaby was a man of slight build and wore round-shaped spectacles. If a ritual required a special task, he was always the one to get called upon for help. He didn't seem to be overly excited about participating in the ritual, but what he lacked in enthusiasm, he more than made up for in dedication. Barnaby got up from his seat and shuffled up to the gong which was located by the entrance to the sanctuary. He struck it twice then slowly made his was back to his seat. The audience stood up quietly and waited for further instructions. And then the major led the membership in the Owl pledge of allegiance.

I pledge allegiance
To God and country
To fight for freedom
And protect our ways.
Bonded by blood
We will vanquish our enemies
From highland to lowland
And from shore and shore.
Hear us, our brothers and sisters
Hear us, our children
The English Owls of Manchester
Shall always watch over you.
God save our country!
God save the Queen!

After the pledge, everyone took to their seats in anticipation of the major's address to the assembly.

"At this midnight hour, in this great sanctuary, amongst this distinguished audience of honorable Owls, we have come together to bear witness to the formal induction of a new member into the English Owls of Manchester!"

The entire membership stood up and broke into unbridled applause and bellowed out a constant torrent of hooting and hollering. The major raised his hands and encouraged the rowdy audience to continue their merrymaking.

The major yelled out to the crowd, "Lay it on me, baby!!" causing the crowd to erupt in an enthusiastic frenzy. Everyone stood up and chanted the refrain, "Oh-oh-ohhh, oh-oh-ohhh, oh-oh-ohhh, oh-oh-ohhh." This went on for several minutes before the major pounded the gavel a couple times and the chanting gradually faded. The audience ended the uproar with the quick flourish, "Hi-de-hi, hi-de-ho. Ha-ha-ha! Ho-ho-ho!"

The major motioned for everyone to sit down, and he continued with the introduction.

"My dear friends, I present to you the candidate, Jonathan Henry Curtis and his sponsor, the honorable Charles Haywood Grisham III!"

The entire congregation stood up, clapped, and hooted. The major pounded his gavel, and when the applause stopped he continued with his address.

"Yes, ladies and gentlemen, this man, this young man, once a kindergarten baby, born in the gravy, tender and mild, molded and sculpted from saffron, honeysuckle, and buttercups, has come before us to plead his desire to become one of us. In this brief, but fulfilling moment, precious and significant, momentous and illustrious, we have a candidate who wishes to enter this special sanctum of people and things, great and powerful, energized, quantified, and unified in harmonious equilibrium that is reserved solely for those of noble pursuits. This is the place and this is the time for the mystical transformation of a man and his conscience. It's been a long journey for this young man which is about to culminate in a new beginning."

The major paused from his speech and looked at me with fatherly pride and exclaimed, "Oh, yes, Mr. Curtis, this is where it's at!" Then he smiled and shouted, "You've come a long way, baby!!"

The Owls went crazy after hearing the major lay on the praises to me and they started chanting in unison, "Go, baby, go! Go, baby, go! Go, baby, go! Go, baby, go!" After a few minutes of chanting, the major pounded his gavel a couple times and the audience immediately became silent.

"Yes! Yes! Yes!" the major shouted. "Yowza!! Let's get this show on the road! Hooooo!!!"

Everyone stood up and started making three repetitive quick claps in unison, just like they do at sporting events. This went on for another minute or so, and when the gavel was heard again, the clapping immediately ceased. The major adjusted his glasses and turned toward Charles and me.

"Will you both please stand?"

Charles and I stood up and faced the major.

"I will now have Barnaby Beale bring up the holy bible!" the major announced to the crowd.

Barnaby got up from his seat and made his way toward the center of the room where he handed the bible to the major. Upon returning to his seat he could be heard grumbling to himself, "Barnaby do this, Barnaby do that. I do all the work around here and what do I get out of it? Nothing!"

The major looked at Charles and called out to him, "Mr. Grisham, please step forward!"

Charles approached the major and stood in front of him.

"Raise your right hand and place your left hand on the bible." Charles complied as requested and the major continued. "Do you, Charles Haywood Grisham, solemnly swear that the person you bring before us tonight is of sound mind and spirit, and of good heart, and does not possess any evil intentions or fraudulent interests?"

"I do."

"Please introduce the candidate for induction," the major asked Charles.

"I present to you and to this gathering, Jonathan Henry Curtis!"

"Thank you, Mr. Grisham. Please remain standing." The major looked at me and called out in a loud voice, "Jonathan Henry Curtis, please step forward!" I followed the major's instructions and stood in front of him.

"Mr. Curtis, you have been selected as a candidate to be received as a full member into the English Owls of Manchester. This is a big responsibility, young man. When you become one of us, you become a member of a special family that has served communities around the world for over 800 years. And you wouldn't just become an ordinary run-of-the-mill sort of Owl. No! You would become a highly esteemed English Owl!" The major gave me a serious look. "Mr. Curtis, do you come here of your own free will and not by coercion or intimidation?"

"Yes."

"Are you engaged in any sort of espionage of which this group is a target?"

"No."

"If you're having second thoughts about joining us, now is the time to make your feelings known. We do not wish to bestow membership upon someone who is unsure of his willingness to become an Owl. If this is the case, you are free to go and there will be no hard feelings. Therefore, do you wish to walk out that door as a commoner, or is it your desire to remain here and take the oath and become an esteemed English Owl?"

"I wish to remain here and take the oath."

"Are you sure?"

"Yes, I'm sure."

"Then let it be recorded that the candidate has clearly and succinctly expressed his desire to become one of us!" The major raised his fist and shouted, "Let's go Owls!" And the audience responded with the Owl cheer:

Hit 'em high!

Hit 'em low!

Show 'em Owls!

Go! Go! Go!

After the cheering stopped, the major held up the bible and prepared to administer the oath.

"Jonathan Henry Curtis, raise your right hand and place your left hand on the bible." I followed the major's instructions and he continued. "Do you believe in the golden rule?"

"Yes."

"Do you believe in a higher power?"

"Yes."

"Do you denounce the devil and all forms of evil?"

"Yes."

"Will you make yourself available to always help out a fellow Owl in the time of need?"

"Yes."

"Can you keep a secret?"

"Yes."

"Do you swear to uphold and follow all the precepts as written in the Sacred Scrolls of Manchester in the year 1178 AD?"

"I do."

"Do you smoke marijuana?"

"No."

"Are you nice to your mother?"

"Yes."

"Ladies and gentlemen, it is clear that the candidate has passed the test with flying colors!"

Upon hearing the positive outcome, the membership stood up and briefly clapped then sat back down again. The major placed the bible upon the lectern and pulled out a gold-colored medallion from his pocket.

"Mr. Curtis has answered all the questions set before him correctly. I shall now place the Golden Owl medallion around his neck as a gift from all of us." The major stood in front of me and placed the medallion around my neck, then he grabbed a piece of paper from the shelf below the lectern and held it up for all to see. "And here is the official English Owl membership certificate, suitable for framing, which attests to Mr. Curtis' formal induction and recognition as a full member of the English Owls of Manchester. Therefore, with the power vested in me as president of lodge four twenty-two and witnessed by this congregation, I hereby proclaim, that Jonathan Henry Curtis is now a full and proper member of the English Owls of Manchester! You may now give us the official Owl hoot."

I turned around and hollered, "Hoo-hooooo!!"

"Everyone, please welcome our newest Owl member with a hearty hoot!"

The entire Owl congregation shouted, "Hoo-hooooo!!"

The major extended his hand to thank me. "Congratulations, Mr. Curtis. We welcome you and we honor you, sir." Then he turned to Charles and thanked him for sponsoring me. The major went back behind the lectern to make an announcement.

"Everyone, please join us for food and drink in the social hall. May you all leave this place in comfort and in peace and feel the endless love of our creator. Amen. Your honorable president has spoken! These proceedings are now closed!" The major pounded the gavel and everyone started to exit the sanctuary. I just stood there in a daze, not totally aware of what had just happened. It was one of the strangest ceremonies I had ever participated in, let alone been to.

"Congratulations, Johnny! You did a fantastic job!"

"Thank you, Charles."

"Ahh! Here come the others!"

"Congratulations, Johnny!"

"Thanks, Veronica."

"You were sure a trooper standing up there in front of everyone," she said.

"Well, I did my best."

"You sure did!" she said.

"Well done, Johnny!"

"Thank you, Percy."

"You're one of us now!" he shouted with joy. "How does it feel to be an Owl?"

"Great!"

I couldn't believe how excited everyone was for me. I knew I wanted to become an Owl, but everyone carried on like it was the coronation of a British monarch.

"Let's all go out and celebrate!" Charles said.

"I heard they have food in the social hall."

Percy shook his head. "It's all substandard, Johnny. We need to get some real food, right, Charles?"

"Right!"

"Won't the major get mad?"

"Ah, he'll be good and drunk before you know it, so I wouldn't even worry about it," Charles said.

"Where should we go?" Veronica asked.

"We should go to a place where only Owls are allowed," Percy suggested.

"Why?" I asked.

"Because you're an Owl!"

Charles nodded his head in agreement. "Percy's right, Johnny. You don't have to hang around riff-raff anymore."

"I never did."

Veronica shook her head at my response like I just didn't get it. "C'mon, Johnny, let's go. You have so much to learn," she said.

"Hoo-hoooo!" Percy shouted. "Johnny, why aren't you hooting?"

"I don't feel like hooting right now. I hooted earlier."

"You've got to get with the program, man! Anytime's a good time to hoot," Percy said.

"Let's go, you guys," Charles said. As we headed out, he put his arm around me and spoke to me softly, "Don't worry, Johnny, I know it's all new to you, but in time, we'll turn you into a proper Owl yet."

We went to the Starlight Diner on Beverly Boulevard to celebrate. It didn't appear to be an Owl hangout, but my friends were certain that it was and also told me that the restaurant was in fact Owl owned. Things hadn't all sunk in yet, but I felt proud and carried myself with more confidence than ever, and my friends were happy that I was now one of them.

We stayed out late and drank our fair share of fancy alcoholic drinks while feasting on the most delectable foods. I didn't get home 'til 3:30 in the morning, but once my head hit the pillow, I was off to the world of dreams.

Chapter 8

Hello and Goodbye

I woke up in a great mood and finished three entire scenes of my script. Still feeling giddy about the previous night, I grabbed my cell phone and called Jessica to fill her in the the latest news.

"Hi, Johnny."

"Hey, Jessica! Guess what?"

"You lost weight?"

"No, I'm an Owl!"

"A what?"

"An Owl. I just got initiated into the group last night!"

"Oh, Johnny! Why?"

"What do you mean *why*? It was the chance of a lifetime, and I took it."

"You just joined a cult. Congratulations."

"It's not a cult!"

"Believe what you want."

"There's nothing wrong with the group!"

"I think you're delusional."

"And I think you're jealous!"

"Johnny, we just talked about this a few days ago and you agreed with me."

"Well that was then and this is now."

"What an answer!"

"Well . . . "

I could tell the conversation was going nowhere fast. I couldn't believe how stubborn Jessica was. You'd think that a doctor would be more understanding and not so judgmental.

"You know, Johnny, do what you want, but I don't want any part of it."

"I don't understand why you're making such a big deal about it."

"Look, I don't have time for this right now. I've gotta go."

"Can I come over?"

"Not today, I'm busy."

"Joe Sunday's free."

"Well Joe Sunday will just have to go solo today."

"What about tomorrow?"

"I'm busy tomorrow too. I'll call you sometime when I'm free, okay?

"Yeah, whatever."

"Goodbye, Johnny."

"Bye."

Just because Jessica wasn't an Owl didn't give her permission to be so condescending. And I definitely wasn't going to put up with it. So in retaliation, I stuck my tongue out at the phone and made an obnoxious noise.

Chapter 9

You're one of us Now!

Shortly after I got off the phone with Jessica, I packed an overnight bag and took off on a road trip. A long drive relaxes me, especially after someone gets on my nerves. I decided to head east, but wasn't exactly sure what my destination would be. I just took off and headed down the highway, south on the Four O Five, east onto Interstate 10, and then northeast onto Highway 15 in the direction of the old western town of Barstow. Now I didn't know too much about Barstow other than it being the home to the second largest meteorite ever found in the United States. So this made Barstow seem like a unique place to check out.

About a half-hour into the drive, Charles called. I usually don't like being bothered when I'm trying to relax, but I answered it anyway.

"Hey, Charles."

"Johnny! What's happening?"

"I'm taking a road trip."

"Oh! That's too bad. I thought we could all get together and hang out for the day. When are you getting back?"

"I'm not sure, I'll have to call you."

"Where you at anyway?"

"I'm heading in the direction of Barstow."

"Barstow? Are you nuts? There's nothing in Barstow. It's practically a ghost town!"

"I'm just stopping there for a bit."

"That's just crazy."

"Well you don't have to go!"

"Why I wouldn't set foot in Barstow if you got down on your knees and begged me! Besides, the people in Barstow are not Owl friendly."

"How do you know that?"

"It's common knowledge."

"Well I've never heard that!"

"That's because you're a newbie, Johnny. You're about to enter hostile territory, and now my hands are tied."

"What?"

"I'm afraid your little stunt has crossed the line, so you've really left me no choice. This is definitely a *Code Orange*! I repeat: *Code Orange*!"

"What in the hell are you talking about? What's a *Code Orange*?"

"I can't tell you what it is, but I can assure you it's not good."

Charles was really getting under my skin. Why should he care where I was going? It was really none of his business.

"I want to know what a *Code Orange* is!"

"That's for me to know and for you to find out."

"Look, Charles, I gotta go. I'll talk to you when I get back."

"All right, but don't say I didn't warn you."

"Goodbye, Charles!"

I figured the best way to tune out Charles was to tune the radio for some rock 'n roll, but all I could pick up was a station sending out a series of Morse Code transmissions. After the transmissions ended, a woman came on and started broadcasting a bizarre message. "Attention!

Attention! Friends, lovers, and romantics, lend me your ears: The longing of the heart runs deeply through melancholy fields of sorrows and tears. I repeat: The longing of the heart runs deeply through melancholy fields of sorrows and tears. End of message."

The woman's voice sounded like the person I heard while driving down to San Clemente the other day. The transmission fascinated me and I kept listening to see what the next strange message would be. A few seconds later, some instrumental music came on and the woman started speaking again. "This is Retro Radio Girl coming to you live from the high desert playing the greatest hits from the past."

I knew it! It was the same woman! It was Retro Radio Girl! What a treat it was to hear such a refreshing voice!

"Hey, all you travelers, commuters, and road trippers, I just love talking to you on the radio. You know why? Because no one else loves you more than I do in the whole wide world. So sit back and enjoy some more great music from those lost years of time remembered. Here's one I'm sure you'll really like. Talk to you all later."

The woman's announcement segued into the classic song *An Old Fashioned Love Song* by Three Dog Night. As soon as the song ended, the signal dropped out. "What in the hell happened to the station?" I said to myself. After listening to static for a few minutes, a country music station came on in its place which jolted me out of my seat in displeasure. *Where did Retro Radio Girl go?* I wondered. With a sudden feeling of sadness and longing, I turned off the radio, rolled down my window, and listened to the rustling sound of the dry wind.

A couple hours later I pulled into town and drove slowly down the main drag looking for a place to eat. There wasn't much happening in Barstow, but it wouldn't be fair to compare the place to Las Vegas either. Sometimes a town's character lies hidden away from public view and it's up to the visitor to walk the streets and alleys to uncover it. I was getting near the end of the road when I spotted an old-fashioned diner advertising some good ol' American comfort food. Well I needed no convincing, so I pulled right up to the place.

When I walked up to the diner I noticed a young woman sitting on the curb crying. She must have been in her early 20s and was dressed in torn jeans and an old shirt. She had on a pair of sandals and wore a red-colored bandana around her head. On her right foot was a tattoo of a moose riding shotgun in an old classic Corvette, and on her left forearm was a tattoo of a saxophone with a few musical notes coming out of the horn which I found pretty cool. On the ground in front of her was an over-stuffed pack containing clothes and personal belongings.

"Hey, young lady, are you okay?"

"No, not really."

"Are you hungry?"

"Yeah,"

"Come on, I'll buy you some lunch."

We sat down at the counter and ordered our meals. She began to cry again, so I gave her some tissue and tried to comfort her the best I could. Her name was Alice and she had just left her boyfriend back in L.A. and didn't know what to do.

"What happened?"

"My boyfriend became abusive because I didn't have a job. I couldn't take it anymore so I left him."

"Did he hit you?"

"No, but he was constantly yelling at me and calling me names and said that I was mooching off him. I told him I was looking for a job, but he just kept hounding me."

"How did you get here of all places?"

"I hitchhiked. I was hoping to make it to Vegas."

"What would you do out there?"

"Entertainment. They're always looking for exotic dancers."

"That's not much of a career."

"It's better than getting abused all the time."

Alice started to cry again. She grabbed a napkin from the dispenser on the counter and blotted her eyes.

"Don't worry, things are going to be okay." I grabbed another napkin and wiped away her tears and kept reassuring her that everything was going to be all right even though I really wasn't sure of that myself.

The poor girl must have been starving because when we got our food she gulped it down and didn't utter a word the whole time. I just ate my food in silence and looked at all the shelves filled with antiques that were gathering dust all around the diner. I looked back at Alice and gave her a warm smile. She smiled back and seemed to have calmed down a bit.

"Where do your parents live?" I asked her.

"They live in Brentwood."

"That's a nice area."

"It's all right."

"Can't you stay with them temporarily?"

"I can't go back there!" she shouted back.

"Why not?"

"Because we just don't get along and I haven't talked to them in over a year."

I paused for a moment and gave her a caring look. She pursed her lips and seemed to be getting ready to cry again, but she just stared into space and didn't say anything.

"They must be worried about you."

"I doubt it."

"Let me call them."

"No, please don't. If you give me a little money I can take the next bus to Vegas."

"Las Vegas is not a safe place for a young woman like you."

"Lots of girls go there. I'll be all right. Please, mister, just give me a little money and I'll be on my way."

"Call me Johnny."

"Johnny, just give me some money so I can catch the bus."

"Will you at least let me tell your parents that you're okay?"

"A lot of good that's gonna do."

"Let me try . . . what's the number?"

With a lot of prodding, she finally gave me their number and I called the girl's parents and told them that their daughter was okay. Then after a great deal of persuasion, I managed to put her on the phone with them and they talked for about half an hour. They seemed to get things straightened out enough for Alice to go back home and stay with them for a while. I offered to drive her back to her parent's house and she readily accepted. Just as we were about to head out, she turned to me with a concerned look.

"Johnny, who's that man?" she motioned with her head.

"What man?"

"The man sitting in the booth over there. He just came in and sat down, but he keeps staring at us. I think he even took a few pictures of us with a camera."

"Whaaat? Let me take a look!" And sure enough, there was a man who seemed to be keeping an eye on us while trying to hide his face behind a menu. And then it struck me. "Hey! I know that guy!"

"Who is it?"

"His name's Barnaby. He's an officer at the Owls Lodge I just joined."

"What's an Owl?"

"It's a long story, I'll tell you about it on the way home."

We went over to Barnaby's table and he tried to pretend not to see us. "Barnaby! What are you doing here?"

"Oh, hi there, Johnny," he answered innocently. "I just happened to be in town and thought I'd get a bite to eat."

"You just happened to be in town . . . my foot! You're spying on me!"

"No, I'm not!"

"Yes, you are!"

And then I heard a voice which appeared to be coming from a two-way radio that was clipped onto Barnaby's belt. "2X2M calling 4X4L, 2X2M calling 4X4L, come in." When the transmission ended, there was a short blast of static.

"What are you doing with that radio?" I asked Barnaby.

"Nothing."

Then I heard the same voice coming from the radio again. "2X2M calling 4X4L, 2X2M calling 4X4L, come in."

"Aren't you gonna answer that?"

"Ah, yes, hold on." He picked up the radio, pressed down on the transmission button, and spoke into the radio. "2X2M, this is 4X4L, over."

"4X4L, this is 2X2M, roger. Please report status of Code Orange, over."

"Hey! You are spying on me!" I yelled at Barnaby.

"I wouldn't call it spying; I'm just observing."

Barnaby picked up the radio. "Hold on a minute," he said. "2X2M, this is 4X4L. Subject is at diner cavorting with a young female. Cover has been blown. Repeat: cover has been blown, over."

After hearing what Barnaby just said really got me hot, and just before I could confront him, the voice on the other end began transmitting. "4X4L, this is 2X2M, roger. Return to base and make a full report. 2X2M, over and out."

Barnaby pressed the transmission button and responded. "2X2M, this is 4X4L, roger-roger. 4X4L, over and out."

"Cavorting with a young female?" I asked excitedly."

"Well, I had to say something."

"Who put you up to this?"

"I'm not allowed to say."

"Was it Charles?"

"I'm sorry, Johnny, I took an oath that I would keep any and all secrets."

"Oh, this is too much! You Owls are mad!"

"But Johnny, you seem to forget that you're one of us now."

"Listen, Barnaby, I'm on my own time right now, so stop harassing me." I turned to Alice and said, "Come on, let's get the hell out of here."

"Johnny! Wait!"

"Go home, Barnaby! And make your report, you gutless wonder!"

"But Johnny! he protested."

Alice and I left the restaurant and headed for my car. Barnaby got all flustered and ran after us. "Where are you going?" he demanded.

"None of your business!"

"I shall be reporting this!"

"I don't give a flying fuck what you do! Goodbye, Barnaby!"

As we sped away, Barnaby shouted, "You're a bad Owl!! Ohhh!!! You're a very bad Owl!!!"

Darkness began to fall as we headed back to L.A. I drank a lot of coffee to stay awake, but Alice fell asleep a short distance into the drive. It was probably the best sleep she'd had in a long time. With everything going on, I completely forgot about my unplanned road trip and about checking out the meteorite in Barstow.

I woke Alice up as we entered the Brentwood neighborhood and she helped guide me the rest of the way to her parent's house. I entered the large circular driveway and stopped near the front entrance which was well lit by a pair of porch lights. Just as I had imagined, the place was huge and the yard was immaculately landscaped.

"Call me if you need anything, okay?"

"I will. Thank you, Johnny. You're a sweet man."

Alice gave me a kiss on the cheek, then got out of the car and walked up to the front door where her parents were waiting. After they let her in, we exchanged nods before they went back inside and closed the door.

I headed back home and thought about all the strange events that took place in Barstow. It's funny how things work out. I wonder what would have happened to Alice had I not taken a road trip and stopped at that diner. I often think about things like that. Sometimes all it takes is one split second to have a different outcome. Maybe things are just meant to happen a certain way. But for Alice's sake, I'm glad things turned out the way they did.

Chapter 10

It was all a Misunderstanding!

Pancakes, bacon, scrambled eggs, and lots of coffee was all I needed to get things started in the morning. Even got some walking in to compensate for an old-fashioned chocolate doughnut, but who's keeping track?

Later that morning, Alice called to thank me for helping her get reunited with her parents and for keeping her out of the Las Vegas scene. She told me she was thinking about going back to school and that she would keep me posted. Just after I finished speaking with Alice, Charles called, and I answered it immediately.

"I was just about to call you, Charles," I said sternly.

"Ahh, two minds think alike! The gang's getting together this afternoon; we'll come pick you up at one."

"Hold on, Charles, I'm a little upset right now!"

"What seems to be troubling you, old boy?"

"Barnaby!"

"Nice man, isn't he?"

"What was he doing in Barstow?"

"I don't know. Maybe he was on vacation."

"Nobody takes a vacation to Barstow! He was taking photos of me and communicating with someone over a two-way radio. Did you send him to spy on me?

"Oh, come now, Johnny. Spying is such as strong word."

"Oh, really? Does *Code Orange* mean anything to you?"

"I can't talk about *Code Orange*."

"Why not?"

"It's against the rules."

"What a convenient answer."

"Now look, Johnny, there are some things I just can't discuss—"

"Charles, why was Barnaby there?" I interrupted.

"Well, if you must know, I was concerned for your safety, so I called the major about your road trip and he asked Barnaby to keep an eye on you."

"That makes no sense. Why would my safety be of any concern to you?"

"Because you crossed into enemy territory. Those people have been known to attack Owls and leave them for dead."

"That's insane! I thought the people there were nice."

"That's what they want you to think. They hide in the dark behind trees and bushes, and then, when an Owl least expects it . . . pow! And that's all she wrote."

"I think you're exaggerating."

"Believe what you want, Johnny, but I was really trying to protect you because you're one of my best friends and I didn't want anything to happen to you. That's one of the duties of an Owl; we must always look after one another."

"Look, Charles, I appreciate the thought, but never was I in any danger."

"Well, I'm sorry you took it wrong, ol' chap, but we had nothing but good intentions."

"I'll forget about it this time, Charles, but in the future, no more spying."

"Okay, fine. But if you're ever in danger—"

"I'm not going to be in danger!" I snapped back.

"Well, now that we've got that settled, get yourself ready 'cause we'll be over soon."

"Okay, I'll see you in a bit. Goodbye."

Chapter 11

A Flock of Owls

Since the weather was nice, we decided to go to the Third Street Promenade, an open-air pedestrian only street in Santa Monica filled with intriguing shops and cafes. The Promenade was only a few miles from Jessica's house, but there was no way in hell I was going to spend any time with that mean meanie. Anyways, my friends told me that the Owls should be out in force today and to keep my eyes peeled for any sightings. Percy and Charles tried to educate me on their unique behaviors and what to look for. I attempted to identify some of them, but Percy told me that I was only about 30% accurate. On the other hand, he said that Veronica was picking up the ability to spot Owls on the street rather quickly.

We kept walking down the street with our eyes and ears wide open for any clandestine activity. Charles said he was sensing the presence of Owls and he pointed to an area of the promenade that supposedly had a high concentration of them, but none of us were able to positively identify any members of the group.

"We must try to make contact!" Charles insisted.

"With whom?" I inquired.

"What do you mean *with whom*? We're searching for Owls."

"Are you guys serious?"

67

"You have a lot to learn, Johnny." Someday you'll understand," Percy interjected.

"Understand what?"

Percy shook his head. "In time it will all become clear to you."

"Well tell me now!" I demanded.

"Now's not the time, things could get a little perilous."

"Whaaat?"

Charles gently put his hand on my shoulder and tried to calm me down. "You'd better sit this one out, Johnny."

"Why?"

"There's no time to explain." Charles quickly turned toward Veronica. "Okay, Veronica, get ready."

"I'm ready!" she enthusiastically said.

"Okay . . . now!" Charles yelled.

"Hoo-hooooo!" Veronica shouted.

They stood still for a moment, then Charles looked at her pensively. "Do you hear anything?"

"No, nothing yet," she reported.

Well, Veronica's hoot was apparently not sufficient enough to attract attention. We stood there for about a minute waiting for a response, but no one came forward. I started laughing at the absurdity of it all and tried to convince my friends that it was highly unlikely that a flock of Owls would come out of the shadows and reveal themselves after a prolonged hoot. Yet, Percy took issue with my opinion and said that I was being a typical Aquarian because Aquarians supposedly don't believe in anything.

I laughed and said, "I'm afraid we're the only Owls within miles of here."

"What are you talking about?" Percy said. "Santa Monica's a hotbed for Owl activity."

"Really?" I said with disbelief. "There's a better chance of spotting a vampire than an Owl."

"Don't you have any faith, Johnny? Can't you at least try to believe?"

I didn't answer and just rolled my eyes. Charles told everyone to be quiet and he listened intently as if there was definitely something in the air. He looked at Veronica and made a gesture with his forefinger to be prepared to have another go at it.

"Veronica, try again. This time a little louder, and with more heart," he said.

"I'll do my best, Charles." Veronica got ready, then took a deep breath and let out a big hoot, "Hoo-hooooo!!"

What the hell did I get myself into? And what in God's name happened to my friends? They've turned into a bunch of freaks! I could have been home doing my writing, but instead I was party to some nincompoops trying to establish contact with their allies.

"I don't hear anything, you guys. Maybe Veronica needs to hoot in a higher octave," I teased.

"We'll see who has the last laugh, Johnny. It's just a matter of time before someone finds the courage to come forward," Percy said.

I shook my head and egged them on. "Waiting, wondering, hoping, wishing—"

"Shhhhh! Simmer down, Johnny! I think I might have heard something," Charles claimed.

We all waited in anticipation, but the only sound we heard was the crowd of people strolling the promenade. And then, without warning, a familiar sound filled the air.

"Hoo-hooooo!"

"Hey! Did you hear that? There's an Owl out there!" Veronica shouted with joy.

Percy felt a grand sense of redemption and shook his head in relief. "I knew it! I knew it! See, I told you, Johnny! I told you! Ha! I've been vindicated!"

"That's probably just an imposter pretending to be an Owl," I said flippantly.

"Nonsense, Johnny! Nonsense!" Percy said.

"What an extraordinary phenomenon!" Charles chimed in. "This is deeply satisfying, my friends."

The three amigos continued to believe that we were deep in Owl territory, but I remained skeptical. And then, Veronica prepared to let out another hoot. She tilted her head back, took a deep breath, and shouted, "Hoo-hooooo!!"

"This is crazy!" I said.

Charles raised his hand and lifted his forefinger. "Hold on, Johnny. I can feel something about to happen." And moments later, something did happen.

"Hoo-hooooo!"

"There it is again!" Charles remarked.

"Oh, my God! Oh, my God! They're coming out of the woodwork! "Percy shouted.

"No, they're not!" I said.

Charles and Percy believed they had spotted the person responsible for hooting back at Veronica and waved him over. The suspected Owl walked over to us cautiously from across the promenade. He was a young man of about 18, wearing a baseball cap and eating popcorn from a small paper bag.

"Are you the one who hooted at us?" Percy asked.

"Yes, that was me."

"Fantastic! Simply fantastic! What's your name?

"Bill."

"Well nice to make your acquaintance, Bill! My name's Percy, and this is Johnny, Charles, and Veronica."

We all shook hands with Bill and welcomed him as though he were a long-lost relative from the old country. My friends were ecstatic to learn that a fellow Owl was frequenting the promenade, but I felt it was just a coincidence that he happened to be there. I kept my feelings to myself so as not to cast a shadow on their moment in the sun.

"I'm the one who hooted at you!" Veronica said feeling a sense of accomplishment.

"Great!" Bill said.

"What lodge do you belong to?" Charles asked him.

"Lodge?" What do you mean?"

"You're an Owl, aren't you?"

"An Owl? Are you kidding?"

"Then why did you hoot back at us?"

"I hooted because she hooted."

"Oh, so you're not an Owl then," Charles said.

"Uhh, no, I'm afraid not."

"Sorry for the confusion, young man, but we thought you might have been a fellow member of one of the local Owl lodges."

"Oh, that's quite all right."

"Well, nice hooting at you anyway," Charles said.

"Likewise," the young man said, and he walked back to the other side of the street and started to eat his popcorn again.

Percy appeared to be disappointed, but quickly shrugged it off and put a positive spin on the experience.

"We were so close, my friends! But not to worry, there are definitely Owls out there! I just know it! It's only a matter of time before they come out from hiding. So stay alert everyone, and don't abandon the ship. It could be any second now!"

"Meow!!"

"What was that?" Percy wondered.

"Sounded like a cat," Charles said.

"Meow!!"

Percy became startled. "It is a cat!"

"Two cats! Let's get out of here!" Charles said with anxiety.

A man and a woman rushed over to us from across the street. They were both wearing black slacks and white t-shirts with an image of a cat on the front and the word *Meow!* on the back.

"Not so fast, Owls!" the man said.

"Yeah! Not so fast, Owls!" the woman repeated.

"Who are you guys?" Charles asked.

"I am Lazarus! 4th Degree Knight of the Irish Cats of Galway!"

"And I am Penelope! Lady Squire of the Irish Cats of Galway!"

"What do you cats want?" Charles inquired.

"You're hanging around our turf and we don't like it!" Lazarus warned. "The Promenade is not a place for Owls, so you'd better scram before I call for reinforcements."

"Yeah, ya better get out of here if you know what's good for ya," Penelope added.

"All right, we'll get out of here," Charles said.

"And just remember: Longy McGinnis doesn't like English Owls loitering on our territory! And I wouldn't get Longy mad or there might be trouble," Lazarus said.

"All it takes is one call to Longy and they'll be a rumble," Penelope added.

Charles said that he'd never even heard of Longy McGinnis, but Lazarus explained to him that Longy doesn't associate with Owls, so there was no way he would have heard of him. Charles wasn't happy with this explanation and disputed their claim over the Promenade. But Lazarus countered that any disagreements had to be taken up with Longy and told us to beat it while we still had the chance. Penelope piled on and warned us that they wouldn't be so nice next time.

Veronica got upset and wasn't going to be intimidated. "Charles, you're not going to let them chase us out of here, are you?"

"We could be outnumbered, better safe than sorry," he said.

"Charles is right," Percy said. Those Irish Cats always have something up their sleeves. Now's not the time to take chances. Best to choose our battles wisely. Come on, you guys, let's go.

"Wait a minute! I'm not going anywhere!" I said in anger.

"Don't try to be a hero, Johnny. It's not worth putting yourself in danger."

"I don't care! I'm going to try reasoning with them."

"Are you crazy?" Charles said. "You can't have a constructive conversation with an Irish Cat!"

"Hey, Penelope!" I called out.

"Yeah, what do you want, Owl?"

"What's your number?"

73

"Why do you want to know?"

"So I can ask you out on a date."

"I'm not that easy, Mr. Owl."

This exchange got Lazarus angry. "Hey! What's the big idea?"

"Just trying to be friendly, that's all."

"You've got some nerve, mister."

"Take it easy, Lazarus, I can handle myself," Penelope said. Then she turned back to us and made a threat. "You guys better get going before we make mincemeat out of you."

"Yeah, you and who else?" Veronica shouted.

As Charles tried to calm Veronica down, I handed Penelope my business card and suggested that we get together sometime.

"Johnny, have you lost your mind? She's a Cat!" Charles scolded me.

"So what!"

"Listen to me, Johnny, you don't want to get mixed up with a Cat, it's dangerous!"

"Your friend is right, you'd better listen to him," Lazarus concurred.

Veronica was getting tired of the whole standoff and relented. "C'mon everyone, let's blow this popsicle stand."

Before I turned to leave, I extended another olive branch to Penelope. "Call me!" I said.

"Don't count on it!" she shouted back.

As we headed out, I began to re-examine my affiliation with the Owls and my relationships with my friends. I was getting tired of all the absurd rules and restrictions concocted by the Owls, and I was afraid that my friends were losing touch with reality. They were taking this whole

Owl thing way too seriously and I tried to tell them so, but they wouldn't listen to me. I just closed my eyes and shook my head in disbelief. When I opened them, I saw an old familiar face approaching me.

"Johnny! Johnny Curtis! How are you, my friend?"

"Willy! Hi! I'm doing great. Good to see you! What brings you out here today?"

"Just out for an afternoon stroll, enjoying the weather. What about you?"

"Doing the same, just enjoying the day."

"Well, I've got to go meet up with my wife. Call me soon and let's get together."

"Sounds good, I will."

"Great! See ya, Johnny."

"See ya, Willy."

As the man walked away, Charles approached me. "Johnny, who was that?"

"An old friend."

"Is he an Owl?"

"I don't know. I doubt it."

"Oooh, that's not good," Veronica said.

"Why? I asked."

"He's an outsider."

"What are you talking about? He's a good friend of mine!"

"Yeah, but he's not an Owl."

"So?"

"Look, Johnny, what Veronica's trying to say is that it may be best not to associate with people who are not Owls," Charles said.

"Why not?"

"They can't be trusted."

"Oh, come on! You've got to be joking."

"Johnny, we never joke about such things."

"You know, you guys are a bunch of bigots! I've had enough for one day! I wanna go home now."

"Calm down, Johnny. You're taking it all the wrong way."

"No, I'm not Charles. Now take me home!"

"We were all gonna go out for dinner."

"You can count me out! I'll take a cab home. Goodbye!"

I walked off at a brisk pace and didn't look back.

"I'm sorry, Johnny, please don't go!" Veronica pleaded.

"Ah, let the baby has his way! He's not really an Owl anyway!" Percy said loudly to make sure I heard him. "Come on, you guys, let's go!"

Chapter 12

Sugar and Spice

The moment I got home I fixed myself a strong drink and watched reruns of old black and white TV shows. I find it helpful to get all liquored up when I'm having one of those days. For most people, having one drink is enough, but when you've got friends like mine, it can take several drinks to unwind.

I relaxed in my recliner with a drink in one hand and the TV remote in the other. To my delight, the Honeymooners came on, and just when Ralph Kramden entered his apartment, there was a knock on my door.

"Oh, God! Who is it now?" I said to myself.

"Hi, Johnny."

"Piper! What brings you over here?"

"I just came over to borrow some sugar."

Piper was my next door neighbor. Young, beautiful, late 20s, long blonde hair, great smile, and jam-packed with red-hot energy. She would usually pop in for a visit once a week and just hang out.

"Come on in, the sugar's in the kitchen."

"You know I didn't come over for sugar. Bring us some wine and let's recline."

Piper plopped herself down on my couch and removed her shoes. She obviously wasn't going anywhere for a while.

And she gave me that look as though she was expecting something else from me, a look I knew all too well.

"It looks like you've been drinking," she said.wd

"Just a little bit."

"I'd say a lot. I'd say that you're pretty well drunk."

Piper was good at reading people. Of course, it's not that hard to tell if someone's been drinking.

"Well, maybe I'm a little drunk," I told her.

"Then it should be easy for me to take advantage of you."

She was right. I could never resist Piper. Even if I was completely sober I would still give in to her advances. What red-blooded man wouldn't want to be taken advantage of by a young woman in her prime?

"Come over here, Johnny. Come over here right now!" she ordered.

I sat down next to her and started stroking her arms, and then her legs. She gave me a prolonged kiss that seemed to last forever, and I kissed her back like a good man should. Her eyes enchanted me, her lips enticed me, and her body entrapped me. Oh, that Piper! That young, vivacious, irresistible Piper! She did it to me again, and there was no going back. And she knew it. So she removed her clothing and lied on her back with a smile.

"You know what I want you to do," she said.

"Right now?"

"You've got exactly three seconds to get into position, mister! And I expect a spectacular performance out of you; it's part of being a good neighbor, you know. And if you do a good and proper job, I'll reciprocate the favor . . . deal?"

I managed to muffle out a response. "Mmm hmm."

"I can't hear you!" she said.

"Deal!" I blurted out.

"That's enough talking. Get back down there! Ohhh!"

The close bond of an amorous encounter is the closest of all encounters. Lyrical, rhythmic, primal, bopping the beat and beating the body, rumbling on glistening grains of soft petals, with a slide here and a glide there, draining the sweet fragrant essence of the flowering Southern Magnolia in springtime. But time is lost. No one would even know the time during a jaunt in a wind-swept hidden meadow when you ain't wearing no clothes and no socks unless you're wearing a large, luminous wristwatch with a second hand movement. But there ain't no watches when you're loving your lover. Hell! Nobody gives a rat's ass what time it is anyway!

I lied on my couch in a dreamy state, tranquil and satisfied, barely able to keep my eyes open as Piper slowly dressed. We spoke to each other in our own way, on our own terms, unfiltered and unfettered.

Me: "We embraced, we caressed, we loved."

She: "We got it on. It was lust, pure and simple."

Me: "I felt a certain closeness and bond that only the two of us could know."

She: "I ravaged his entire body like the inside of a ripe mango."

Me: "My mind drifted off in her firm and determined grip."

She: "My head writhed from side-to-side until I shuddered and exploded in ecstasy."

Me: "I was breathless. I recovered in her arms, I drifted off to sleep."

She: "I came, and I went."

Me: *"I was lost in a dream. There was still liquor left in the goblet. Piper . . . Piper . . . draw me toward you and quench my thirst."*

She: *"Goodnight, sweet prince. May hosts of angels sing you to sleep."*

I slept peacefully and forgot all my troubles. An hour with Piper washed away my memories of an entire day of people gone mad in a big and crazy world.

Chapter 13

Love knows no Time

When I got up the following morning, I thought about a girl from Long Island that I hadn't seen in years. We used to hang out all the time, taking the train into the city to explore the different neighborhoods, visiting the main library on Fifth Avenue, going to Coney Island to ride the roller coaster and play skeeball. Other times it was hitting the beaches in the Hamptons or heading up to Montreal for bagels and smoked meat. We did everything together and I miss those days. They were good ol' days 'cause life didn't get in the way yet. So I sat down at my writing desk and wrote her a letter in long hand.

Dear Anna,

It's been a long time since I last saw you, listening to your record albums and eating your fantastic grilled cheese sandwiches with lots of crunchy potato chips and dill pickles on the side and reminiscing about our younger days. I remember all those posters you had up in your bedroom. Do you still have the one with the Captain and Tennille? I think the Carpenters poster was my favorite with those psychedelic clothes they were wearing. I wanted it, but you wouldn't give it to me. Ha! That's okay, wouldn't know where to put it anyway, and I don't think grownups put music posters up in their rooms anymore. I'm still here in L.A., that vast cultureless wasteland with no good bagels and no good pizza. We've got a lot of freeways though, haven't been on them all and don't yet know where they all go, but they must go somewhere. With all the traffic, it takes forever to get anywhere. Everyone here's trying to make it in show biz. It's a tough racket and most people end up going back home 'cause the rent's too high. I know the rent's high in New York too, but at least you can move to Jersey, not that Jersey's anything special. How's your mom doing? Does she still write a column for the paper? I've made lots of friends out here, they're kind of weird, but we've definitely had some good times together. The sunshine's been a good remedy for my depression and I've been off the meds for a few years now. The shrink says I've been making lots of progress, but of course, he's been saying that for the past six years. He's kind of like the shrink I had back in

Manhattan, with the same little couch and the same little writing pad and the same kind of responses like So how do you feel about that? Such originality! I don't think I'm quite ready to come back to New York yet, maybe next year. When I'm ready, you'll be the first to know. I can't believe you've been gone for ten years now! Jeez, Anna, what the hell happened to all the time? Anyway, I think about you a lot, and I'll come visit you soon.

Love,

Johnny

I placed the letter in my desk drawer with all the other letters I wrote to her. And then, leaning back in my chair, I closed my eyes and drifted off for a while. About an hour later, I heard a knock at the door and went to answer it.

Chapter 14

Throwing Caution to the Wind

"Hello, Johnny."

"Penelope! How did you find out where I lived?"

"Connections."

"Come in!" I said happily. "I thought you didn't like Owls."

"I figured a little diplomacy couldn't hurt."

"What about Lazarus?"

"Oh, he'll go crying to Longy and make a big scene, but I don't give a shit. He'll eventually get over it. When I see something I'm interested in, I just go for it, you know what I mean, Johnny?"

"Yeah, I know exactly what you mean. Can I get you a drink?"

"A gin and tonic would be nice."

"Comin' right up!"

I fixed us a couple drinks and we went into the living room. Penelope took a few sips of her drink and began browsing through my books that lined the room in tall cherrywood bookcases. She pulled a book from one of the shelves and started thumbing through it, then placed it back and gave me a coy smile as she slid her forefinger across the spines of several books.

"You have very eclectic tastes," she remarked.

"I take an interest in a lot of different subjects. It's healthy to have an open mind about things."

Penelope smiled and said, "I like people who are open-minded. It makes life a lot more interesting, don't you think?"

"Yes, I think the same way."

Penelope finished her drink and slowly walked around the room admiring all the knick-knacks and collectible items I had. She told me I had a good eye for antiques and that they complemented the room nicely.

"How 'bout another drink?" she asked. "Make it a double this time."

I went back to the kitchen to fix us some more drinks. The spontaneity of Penelope showing up at my door gave me a big rush and I couldn't wait to see how things would transpire. The phone rang and I excused myself for a moment.

"What is it, Charles?"

"Johnny, we're needed."

"What?"

"We're needed to testify at the Meeting of the Minds."

"What in the hell are you talking about?"

"We're having a sit-down with the Irish Cats to air our differences. The meeting's at an old warehouse in Redondo Junction. I'll pick you up in an hour."

"I can't go. I've got company now."

"An Owl has an obligation to support his friends."

"I happen to be with a friend right now."

"Do I know this person?"

"You've seen her before."

"Is she an Owl?"

"No, she's not an Owl, she's a Cat!"

"Nooooo!"

"Yesssss!"

"Penelope?" He asked.

"Penelope has a thing for Owls," I said.

"This is totally unheard of, Johnny! You're breaking all the rules!"

"Goodbye, Charles. May the Owls bless you and keep you." I said sarcastically.

When I came back to the living room, Penelope was sitting on the couch. I handed her a drink and sat down next to her. She took a sip then placed her drink on the coffee table in front of us. Then she took the drink out of my hand and also placed it on the coffee table. And that's when things started to get really exciting. When I went in for a kiss, she playfully pulled her head back then placed her hand on my leg.

"Let's go make love in your backyard!" she said.

"Really? This is an apartment complex, you know, and a lot of windows face the greenbelt."

"So?"

"And the fence isn't very high either."

"No one's gonna see us! It looks fairly secluded to me."

"I don't know . . ." I said hesitantly.

"Where's your sense of adventure?"

"Hey! You're looking at Mr. Adventure himself! But there are limits to how far one should go."

"Johnny, adventure's not about limits, it's about taking risks and reaping the rewards."

"Yes, but not unnecessary risks."

"It's not like we're scaling a steep mountain without any rope; we're talking about having sex in a semi-private setting where anything can happen, and that's what makes it all the more enticing. Sex is much more exciting when there's a little danger involved. C'mon, let's do it!"

Her reasoning was a little flawed, but I agreed to go ahead with her idea. So we grabbed a large towel and set out for the backyard. We laid out the towel on the soft grass and removed our shoes and socks. Now that part was easy to do, and the grass felt good under our bare feet and we quickly began to make out. She removed her shirt and bra, and I instinctively caressed her breasts with my hands and mouth. We stripped off the rest of our clothing and things got a whole lot steamier.

The kissing, the touching, and the caressing raised the intensity level of our intimate indulgence, encouraging us to satisfy the hidden, passionate voices yearning to be acted upon. The moment she climbed on top of me, a tall order, but attainable, I closed my eyes and immediately forgot about my surroundings. With all inhibitions lost and all anxiety removed, I was able to fully let go and enjoy the moment. Penelope kept moving at a steady pace and I kept tying to hold on for dear life and make things last just a little longer. And just when I thought I was about to lose control, I felt a gentle tap on my shoulder. When I opened my eyes, I saw the smiling face of my next-door neighbor.

"Well, well, what have we here? Just couldn't get enough, huh, Johnny?"

"Piper!"

"I've been watching you guys, and I like what I see. I hope you don't mind me joining in."

No, nobody minded. Nobody minded in the least. Penelope was unphased and welcomed our young guest to the party. And in a New York minute, Piper was out of her clothes and displayed a ripened readiness to become all tangled up in a twisted pile of locked limbs and fiery flesh. There were no words to describe the things we did nor the sounds we uttered, there were just natural and spontaneous variations of sexual activity comprising rhythmic and sustained movement for maximum effect.

After going the distance, we rolled off one another for a moment, and then repositioned ourselves into a different configuration. What endless possibilities! What endless dreams! Our thoughts mingled in blissful serenity:

Me: "How did you recognize my desire for romantic intrigue? Was it the words I said? Was it my smile? Or was it the gleam in my eye?"

Penelope: "There are no secrets when it comes to a man's need for sustenance. His intentions cannot stay buried for long. They always rise to the surface like the frothy head of a pint of sparkling amber ale. And then, at the appropriate time, all senses awaken when the bell in the clock tower tolls."

Me: "Is there any harm in having too much of a good thing?"

Piper: "Excess is a matter of interpretation. When it comes to passion, you can never have too much of a good thing. And if I may be so bold to speak for most men: there is no such thing as having too much pussy."

Me: "The ways of love is a physical love. It all comes from our need to kiss and be kissed."

Penelope: "Graze upon my lips, and if those hills be dry, stray lower, where the pleasant fountains lie."

Piper: "My cherry lips have often kissed thy stones. Thy stones with lime and hair knit up in thee."

Me: "You have enlightened me as to the ways of love. Let it be known to lovers loved of my renaissance of love

and my understanding of young Cupid's fiery arrow
quenched in the chaste beams of the watery moon."

After losing ourselves in a lustful daze, we got up to retrieve our clothes and were greeted with enthusiastic applause from the tenants observing from their balconies. We were not shaken, nor were we ashamed from our moment of sexual fulfillment. Penelope was right; taking risks does have its rewards. I don't think I'll ever be able to measure the amount of satisfaction I received from our impromptu lovemaking session. I would do it again in a heartbeat, no matter what the risks were.

After a final embrace, Penelope and Piper left the premises, and I went inside and lied down on my bed and contemplated all that had just happened. I fell asleep and dreamed good dreams like the ones I used to have as a young child after a long day of play in a long-lost world of fantasy and exploration.

Chapter 15

A Case of Moral Turpitude

There's nothing better than having a good night's sleep after making it with two beautiful women, and there's nothing worse than having the phone ring in the middle of a pleasant dream.

"Hello?"

"Hello, Mr. Curtis?"

"Yes?"

"My name's Chatsworth. We haven't become acquainted yet, but I'm the chairman of the English Owls Enforcement Division. I've been instructed by Major Grimsby to inform you that your presence at the lodge is required within the hour."

"Whaaat? For what reason?"

"For reasons which cannot be divulged at this moment."

"Do you know what time it is? It's 4:00 in the morning!"

"I am well aware of the time, Mr. Curtis. In this case, the time is irrelevant. You seem to forget that you're an Owl now."

"Do you realize that I'm half asleep and can't keep my eyes open?"

"Ahh, but Mr. Curtis, Owls never sleep."

"Well this Owl needs his sleep, so if you'll excuse me, I must be going–"

Chatsworth interrupted me before I could hang up the phone. "You're being most uncooperative, sir! I must tell you that the situation is quite serious and that you must present yourself before the board of questioning."

"Listen, Chatsworth, I don't know who you are, or what you want; I take orders from no one. My time's my own; call me back at a decent hour."

"Now look here, Mr. Curtis!—"

"Ah, go peddle your papers!"

"The major shall be hearing about this!"

"Goodbye, Chatsworth!"

"What is the matter with these people?" I said to myself. "Let me sleep for God's sakes!" I drifted off again and found myself in a place far from home, yet familiar in some unexplained way. That's the nature of dreams, they come to us unannounced and take us away without asking. They know we can't control them, but that's none of their concern. Their job is to make sure we go just beyond the contours of understanding, where memories are fragmented and faces are disguised, in a journey that cannot be retraced or redrawn, where we are forever clamoring to be sent back home, but can never get there because the road going back never ends.

The phone rang again. "Whaaat?" I yelled out to myself.

"Hello?"

"Mr. Curtis?"

"Yes?"

"Do you know who this is?"

"You sound like the major."

"Only my friends call me that, and right now I'm not so sure you're my friend."

"Why are you calling?"

"I just received a disturbing phone call from Chatsworth that you were mean to him."

"I wasn't mean to him; I had a long night and was tired."

"You abruptly hung up on him!"

"I wanted to get back to sleep."

"Owls never sleep!"

"Well if you want to stay up all night, that's your prerogative. This Owl's going to bed and sleeping in!"

"You'll do nothing of the kind! I'm the president of the English Owls and it's most urgent that you come to the lodge immediately and respond to the charges leveled against you!"

"What charges?"

"That you knowingly and willfully had certain dealings with a female member of a rival group."

"What do you mean *dealings*?"

"Now's not the proper time to go into it. You must appear at the lodge and undergo a complete and thorough investigation into a series of acts which could amount to high treason."

"Treason?"

"I'm afraid so, Mr. Curtis. So put on your coat and get down to the lodge this instant."

"No. I won't go. You hear me, I won't go! You'll have to get your entertainment somewhere else!"

"Oh, but you will, Mr. Curtis. An Owl must always obey his superiors."

"Hey, major, the last train leaves at noon . . . be under it!"

"Oh, dear! This amounts to moral turpitude! I'm afraid we may have to reconsider your membership in the English Owls."

"Look, right now I don't give a rat's ass!"

"You said the word *ass*! This is very distressing indeed! You're on shaky ground, Mr. Curtis. You just could be the first person to ever have his Owl membership rescinded!"

"Who gives a shit?" I yelled back.

"You just violated our code of ethics. I shall be taking this up with the rules committee first thing. I am now terminating this unpleasant conversation."

The major hung up the phone on me, and I said to myself, "The nerve of that guy! Get a life!" I tried my best to not let that bird-brained fat ass get me upset, and I went to bed to get some sleep. And wouldn't you know it? A half-hour later the phone rang again. "This is getting fucking ridiculous!" I cried out.

"Yes, Charles. What is it?"

"Johnny, what's the matter with you?"

"Nothing's the matter with me!"

"The major just called all upset. He was beside himself."

"I think you're exaggerating."

"He was literally crying on the phone. You can't talk to the major that way!"

"Oh, please!"

"I risked my reputation to get you into the Owls! And this is how you repay me?"

"Charles, this has nothing to do with you."

"I vouched for you, Johnny. Not only were you rude to the major, you could be charged with treason for sleeping with the enemy. After all that has happened, I have serious doubts that we can remain friends."

"Charles, the Owls is a cult, and I want no part of it!"

"How dare you call it a cult! How dare you!!"

"It's a cult, Charles."

"No, it's not!"

"Yes, it is!"

"It's not!"

"It is!"

"This is not going to go over very well," Charles said in a serious tone."

"Well, I don't care."

"You've got a long row to hoe, Johnny! A long row to hoe!"

"Goodbye, Charles."

I hung up the phone and turned it off. *What was I thinking?* I thought to myself. *I should never have joined that group!* Any membership in a secret society is like paying for a one-way ticket to hell, only the fire is much hotter.

Chapter 16

Hold fast to Dreams

The best way for me to handle hostile and confrontational people is to get away from them. So I hit the road again without exactly knowing where I'd end up. I just kept going and going, following one highway after another, out into the desert, out in the middle of nowhere. My head was swimming with so many voices and thoughts, so I figured a long drive would do me good and take my mind off things. But with a lack of sleep and not much energy, my drive was anything but peaceful, and that chorus of voices in my head caught me at a vulnerable time.

Percy: "You're one of us now!"

Chatsworth: "Owls never sleep!"

Veronica: "Hoo-hooooo!"

Major Grimsby: "Moral turpitude!"

Charles: "This is definitely a Code Orange!"

Barnaby: "You're a very bad Owl!!!"

Angela: "Fuck you, Johnny!"

Jessica: "Go down on me."

Piper: "Ohhh!"

After riding hard for several miles, the voices in my head finally subsided. I took control of the wheel, burned some rubber, and sped up to a hundred miles an hour like I was on the Indianapolis Motor Speedway. Cars were sparse on the highway, but what cars there were, I raced past them and honked at them and kept going. Man, was I flying! Those wimpy-ass drivers had no chance of catching me! I was a bat out of hell, a maniac on the highway, a cool cat with dark shades on a revved-up V8 pulling 2 Gs out into the stratosphere! Yeah, baby, that was me! So pack up your lunch and ride with the bunch so you don't get caught up in a crunch! Ha-ha!

A hundred and ten degrees and an hour later and not a car in sight! Radio on, sounds of static crashing through the dash, dust devils dancing across the barren landscape; man, I was way out there! All alone on a desert highway, driving on hot sticky asphalt amongst the tumbleweeds and desert sand. Home to the lizards, rattlesnakes and desert squirrels, and even to the lonely Gila monster. I could have been in Death Valley or some other valley, but I had no idea where I was. All I know is that I made it to the middle of nowhere and that was far enough. I stopped the car along the side of the road with the engine running and the air conditioning on high and nodded off and went into a deep, deep sleep, probably deeper than any time in recent memory. About a half-hour into my slumber, I heard a familiar voice coming from the radio.

"Attention! Attention! 525 6362. Attention! Attention! 525 6362. Stand by for message . . . Follow my voice to the edge of the horizon and let me mend your broken heart. I repeat: Follow my voice to the edge of the horizon and let me mend your broken heart."

When the message ended there was dead air, but I kept listening in the hopes that more was to come. And indeed, there was. The music came up and the announcement I had been waiting for filled the airwaves. "Hello, everyone, this is Retro Radio Girl, broadcasting to those who roam the lonesome desert highways. Even if there is only one person listening to me out there, and you know who you are, I want you to know that I care about you more than anyone else in the whole wide world. See you at the end of the highway!"

Oh, how I would love to meet Retro Radio Girl! I thought to myself. *If only I had her number.* I knew that she was broadcasting from several miles away, but it almost seemed as though she was sitting right next to me. I listened intently as she continued her broadcast. "Head east, then south, then east again. It's easy. Just head east, then south, then east again. I'll get you there." I had no idea who this woman was, or even if she was real, but something inside me told me to take a chance and meet her. So I put the car in drive and headed east, and then took the first dirt road to the south, and the next dirt road to the east. The road narrowed and the ride became quite bumpy. I didn't know where I was; there was absolutely nothing out there. And then it hit me! I stopped the car and sat there silently. That number she was reading; that was my old phone number! It could be a coincidence, but I think that message was for me.

The woman came back on the air and continued giving directions. "Drive to the end of the road and through the gate and keep going until you enter a green field." I slowly headed down the road again, and just as I was about to pass through the gate, I remembered whose voice that was. I entered the green field, stepped out of my car and saw her walking toward me. The sun was shining in a deep blue sky, and the woman I hadn't seen in years looked as radiant as ever.

"Oh, my God!" I said with disbelief.

She smiled and walked right up to me. "It's been a while."

"Yes, it has. I . . . I thought I wouldn't see you until I . . . am I dead?"

"No, you're not dead, not yet anyway."

"Then I must be dreaming."

"It's up to you how to interpret it."

"Then where am I?"

"It's sort of like a dream, but it's more than that."

"Are you okay?"

"Yes, of course."

"What's it like?"

"Different, but I'm in a good place."

"God, I missed you, Anna! I missed you so much!"

I started crying, but she kept smiling and was reassuring. I could tell . . . no, I could feel that she knew all that I was going through. It was a weird sensation, but it all sort of made sense. I can't explain it.

"Why did you call me?"

"You know the answer to that, Johnny. It's time to move on. What we had was in the past, and you can't live your life by holding onto things that aren't here anymore. You've got to live in the present. There's no other choice."

"I know. I just wanted–"

"You don't need my permission. It's okay. You can stop searching and stop moving from person to person and from place to place."

"I know."

"There's someone who loves you out there, Johnny. Why not take a chance?"

"Maybe someday we–"

"No, Johnny, you need to concentrate on what you have now. That's the best way."

"So you must know what I've been up to."

She smiled and said, "I'm aware of your activities. What's this Owl thing all about?"

"Oh, I kind of got caught up in an unfortunate circumstance. I didn't know it would end up to be so crazy."

"And these young women you hang around, are they that appealing?"

"Well, you know, Anna, I mean, I'm a guy, and that's what guys do sometimes. You're not mad at me, are you?"

"I'm not going to tell you how to live your life, Johnny. Your life is your own. You've got to figure things out your own way in your own time."

"How much time do we have?"

"As much time as you need."

"Can I see you again?"

"You won't need to."

"But it'll be hard not to remember this moment and not want to see you."

"You'll remember this moment in much the same way as a dream."

Anna looked at me and smiled. "Okay, Johnny?"

"Okay, Anna."

"Be honest, be true to yourself, and treat others with dignity and respect. Do these things and you'll find your time here to be more satisfying."

"Thank you, Anna. I love you."

"I love you too, Johnny. Oh, and one thing more . . . "

"What?"

"Stop writing me all those damn letters!"

"Okay."

"And if you really want my posters, my mom still has them in her garage."

"I don't need them."

"I didn't think so. Goodbye, Johnny."

"Goodbye, Anna."

I began to walk toward my car, then turned around. "By the way, where did you come up with this Retro Radio Girl routine?"

"I had to get your attention somehow. Did you like it?"

"Yes, I thought it was very creative."

"Maybe you should use it in one of your stories."

"Maybe I will."

"See you, Johnny. Take care of yourself."

"See you, Anna. Thanks. Thanks for everything."

I smiled at her and slowly walked back to my car, knowing that I would never see her again. As I turned the car around, I waved at her and she waved back. I headed through the gate, and when I looked in the rear-view mirror, she was gone.

On my way back to L.A. I felt free and alive and was filled with positive energy. I shouted to the distant mountains, "It's time for me to say goodbye and go somewhere else!" I could tell those mountains wanted to know where I was going, but they just stood there real quiet and all majestic-like. I whispered in the wind that I had a special place in mind and everyone that heard me thought it was a good idea. So I stepped on the gas and let 'er rip and said goodbye to all the little denizens of the desert. And those wisecracking old mountains told me to not let the door hit me on the ass on the way out.

Chapter 17

Welcome back, Johnny Curtis!

"I warned you, Johnny. I told you those groups have bizarre rituals and are made up of people with abnormal behaviors."

"I know."

"So why didn't you listen to me? Why did you have to be so stubborn?"

"I thought it would be kind of cool to belong to an exclusive group."

"But you're not a conformist. You're the type of guy who goes his own way and writes his own ticket. You have principles! If you listen to your heart, you can never go wrong. You should know this more than anyone, you're a writer for God's sakes!"

"Jessica, you seem to forget that writers can sometimes lose their heads too."

"Well, you got out, and that's all that counts."

"But I didn't want to get out. Even with all the warning signs, I wanted to stay. Maybe I'm attracted to the weird and bizarre."

"It's not the end of the world, Johnny."

"Yeah, but you lost a little faith in me."

"You know, Johnny, with all your flaws and all your crazy ideas, it's hard not to like you. You're fun, you're creative, and you make me laugh. And usually that's reason enough for me to want to go to bed with you. The only thing I can recommend is that you cut down on the candy bars. I hope you don't mind my honesty."

Of course, I did mind and tried to tell her so. "That's just what I wanted to talk to you about, Jessica."

"Not now, Johnny. I'm not in the mood to talk. You know, sometimes you just talk too much."

Jessica moved her hand down to my lower extremities and looked into my eyes. "Maybe this will shut you up." She removed her robe, and with a quick and deliberate movement, much like an Olympic gymnast, her body became a lethal weapon and she used it to her full advantage. But I didn't mind, after all the good doctor knows her anatomy like nobody's business.

Chapter 18

Speak to me Polonius!

I came back home in a happy mood and put the finishing touches on my script. Nothing got in the way to distract me; it was just me, my laptop, and a glass of Chardonnay.

A few days after I left the Owls I heard from Charles. He told me that he, Veronica, and Percy had also left the group. Apparently, they too got fed up with all the strange beliefs and peculiar behaviors. He said that our friendship meant much more than belonging to some bizarre club.

I think I knew all along that it's important to follow your heart and not pay much attention to what other people are doing. You've got to live your own life your own way; it's just a matter of staying on the right path.

This above all: to thine own self be true,
And it must follow, as the night the day,
Thou canst not then be false to any man,
Farewell, my blessing season this in thee!

In other words: baby, you've got to be real!

The End

ABOUT THE AUTHOR

Photo by Jenny Nguyen

Kevin Malin was born in Seattle in 1958. After graduating from Central Washington University in 1980, he went into the scrap metal business before deciding to enter the entertainment field. In the late 1990s he studied acting at the Lee Strasberg Acting Workshop and at Freehold Theatre.

In 2002, Malin wrote, produced, and directed his first short film called *The Story of Colette* followed by another short film called *Coffee for Two*. He has written and performed in numerous radio plays and comedy sketches, and has also written and narrated several short stories.

Kevin Malin currently resides in Seattle, and news about his current projects can be found on his website at kevinmalin.com. He can also be reached at kevinmalin@gmail.com.